Faraway Village

Field of Berry Bushes

Enchanted Forest

Milliner's Shop

Fruit Shop

Fairy Ring

Big Trees
(Where Trolls, Giants,
and Dragons Dwell)

The Story of the Leprechaun

By Katherine Tegen • Illustrated by Sally Anne Lambert

HARPER

An Imprint of HarperCollinsPublishers

For Charlotte
—K.T.

For my daughter Katie
—S.A.L.

Library of Congress Cataloging-in-Publication Data
Tegen, Katherine Brown.
  The story of the leprechaun / by Katherine Tegen ; illustrated by Sally Anne Lambert. — 1st ed.
    p. cm.
  Summary: A clever leprechaun who has amassed a pot of gold by making beautiful shoes for people decides to hide his
money at the end of a rainbow, knowing that no one will find it there.
  ISBN 978-0-06-143086-2 (trade bdg.) — ISBN 978-0-06-143085-5 (lib. bdg.)
  [1. Leprechauns—Fiction.] I. Lambert, Sally Anne, ill. II. Title.
PZ7.T22964Sto 2011   2008034358
[E]—dc22   CIP
                                                                                                       AC

Typography by Jeanne L. Hogle
11 12 13 14 15 SCP 10 9 8 7 6 5 4 3 2 1
❖
First Edition

AUTHOR'S NOTE

Leprechauns are a type of fairy, and for that reason they have magical powers and can grant wishes. Most leprechauns live in Ireland, although quite a few came to North America when families left Ireland in the nineteenth century. Leprechauns are misers and are careful about keeping their pots of gold in a safe place. They are generally suspicious of humans, who often try to capture them or trick them in order to get the pot of gold. Unlike humans, they also have a natural ability to find the end of a rainbow, which is handy when burying treasure.

A little man, about two feet tall, lived under a large tree by a stream.

You could easily find him by listening for the *tap, tap, tap* of his hammer.

The little man was a shoemaker.
He spent his days making shoes
that were green-gold and lavender–

some with pointy toes and
some with high heels—
for the people who lived nearby

and for the fairies who lived in the woods.

The people knew he was a leprechaun,
for there were many fairies like him
who lived outside villages.

The people paid the leprechaun
with pieces of gold
for the shoes that he cobbled.

The fairies' shoes were made of satin
and they were tiny.
The fairies brought their gold to the leprechaun too.

The leprechaun needed a place to keep his gold.
He was a bit of a miser,
so he didn't like to spend his money.

An old metal pot became the perfect place
for all of his wealth.

His shoes were so prized that soon
his pot of gold was overflowing.

One day a man named Tim
came to the leprechaun's shop by the tree.

He wanted a pair of shoes
that would be violet-blue with thick heels.

As he was describing the shoes to the leprechaun,
Tim spied the pot of gold.

Tim knew that if he could capture the leprechaun,
he would be granted three wishes
because leprechauns are magic.

"I'll come back in a few days to collect my shoes," said Tim.

The leprechaun was no fool.
He knew what the man was really after.

He buried his pot of gold
in a field filled with berry bushes.

A few days later, Tim came back and
the leprechaun gave him the violet-blue shoes.

But when the leprechaun turned to hide his payment,
he was snatched from behind!

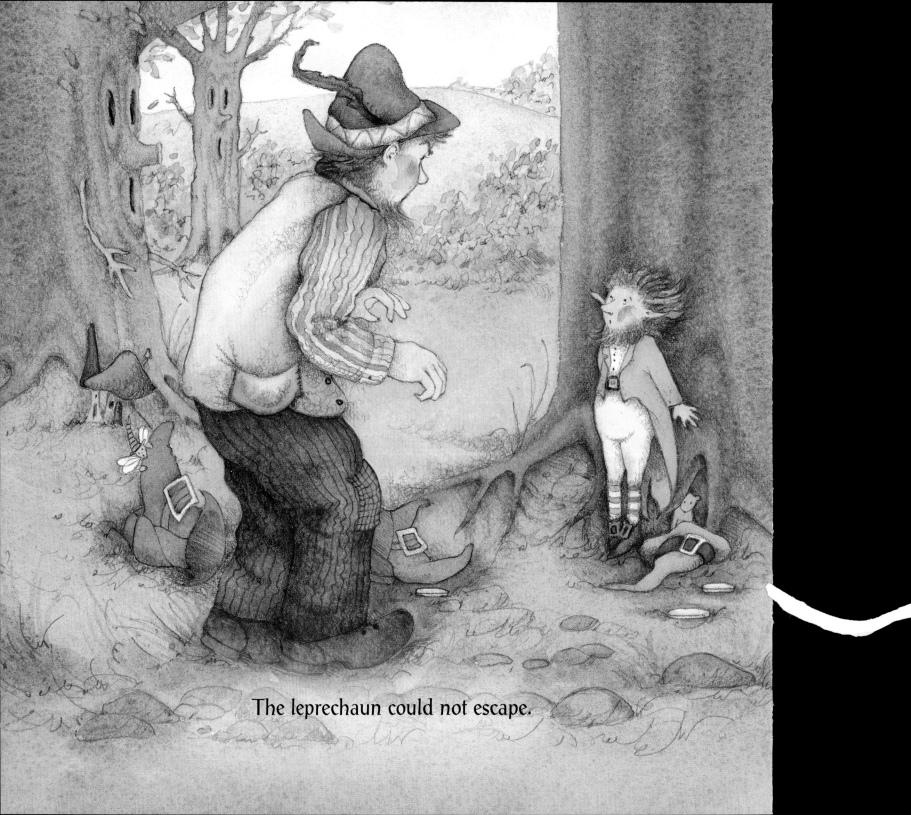

The leprechaun could not escape.

Now Tim could get what he wanted.
"For my first wish, I want you to show me
where the pot of gold is hidden.

"For my second wish,
I want a hundred pairs of shoes.

"And for my third wish,
I want three more wishes."

The leprechaun said, "I can grant you
the first two wishes,
but the third wish is a greedy trick
and cannot be granted."

The leprechaun brought Tim
to the field and pointed to the spot
where the gold was buried.

Tim had no shovel to dig with,
so he marked the spot with a stick and a shoe.
He would come back later.

When Tim returned,
he could not believe his eyes.

There were two hundred sticks
with two hundred shoes
all over the field.

It was leprechaun magic!

Tim dug many holes in the field,
but he couldn't find the spot
where the pot of gold was buried.

After a few hours, he gave up.
When he tried to collect the shoes, each one disappeared.
The leprechaun had tricked him!

The leprechaun needed to find
a better place to hide his gold.

He knew that rainbows were magic.
You could never tell where one ended,
and if he buried his gold at the end of one
only he would know how to find it again.

So that is what he did.

People still try to find his gold,

but they never will.

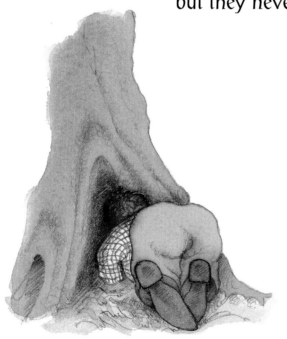

Listen for the sound of the leprechaun—
tap, tap, tap—as he cobbles his shoes.

Perhaps if you find him,
and if you are very nice to him . . .

He will grant you a wish!

Distant Hills

Peat Bogs
(Where Goblins Live)

Bakery

Grocer

Big People's Village

Elfin
Blacksmith

Shoemaker

Stream